by Mary Ellen Friday

Illustrated
by Glin Dibley

It's a
BAD
Day

rising moon

www.risingmoonbooks.com

Composed in the United States of America
Printed in China

Edited by Theresa Howell
Designed by Katie Jennings

FIRST IMPRESSION 2006

ISBN 13: 978-0-87358-904-8
ISBN 10: 0-87358-904-1

06   07   08   09   10   5   4   3   2   1

Friday, Mary Ellen.
It's a bad day / by Mary Ellen Friday ; illustrated by Glin Dibley.
p. cm.
Summary: Children believe that although bad things can happen,
like missing a party because of chicken pox or getting their airplane caught in a tree, their luck may change tomorrow.
ISBN-13: 978-0-87358-904-8 (hardcover : alk. paper)
ISBN-10: 0-87358-904-1 (hardcover : alk. paper)
[1. Luck--Fiction. 2. Attitude (Psychology)--Fiction.]   I. Dibley, Glin, ill. II. Title.
PZ7.F89592It 2006
[E]--dc22
2006007554

To my daughter, Rosa,
with love and thanks
for the inspiration!

— M.E.F.

For Tyler and Kael.

— G.D.

It's a bad day...

when people with BIG hair sit in front of you.

It's a bad day...

when you have to eat brussels sprouts before you can have dessert.

It's a bad day...

when the glue won't glue on the paper.

It's a bad day...

when your favorite t-shirt doesn't fit anymore.

It's a bad day...

when your little sister
practices with scissors
on your best picture.

It's a bad day...

when you blow a world-record-breaking bubble, and it pops before anyone gets to see it.

It's a bad day...

when the dog doesn't want

to go for a walk...now.

It's a bad day...
when the snowman melts.

It's a bad day...

when the tree
eats your airplane.

It's a bad day...

when the skateboard
gets away.

It's a bad day...

when the tattoo
you got as a prize
comes off in
the bath water.

It was a bad day...

But hey, I'm okay.

And tomorrow is
another day.